Mini Marvels

KENT

First published in Great Britain in 2010 by
Young Writers, Remus House, Coltsfoot Drive,
Peterborough, PE2 9JX
Tel (01733) 890066 Fax (01733) 313524
Website: www.youngwriters.co.uk

Disclaimer
Young Writers has maintained every effort
to publish stories that will not cause offence.
Any stories, events or activities relating to individuals
should be read as fictional pieces and not construed
as real-life character portrayal.

Foreword

Since Young Writers was established in 1990, our aim has been to promote and encourage written creativity amongst children and young adults. By giving aspiring young authors the chance to be published, Young Writers effectively nurtures the creative talents of the next generation, allowing their confidence and writing ability to grow.

With our latest fun competition, *The Adventure Starts Here ...* , secondary school children nationwide were given the tricky challenge of writing a story with a beginning, middle and an end in just fifty words.

The diverse and imaginative range of entries made the selection process a difficult but enjoyable task with stories chosen on the basis of style, expression, flair and technical skill. A fascinating glimpse into the imaginations of the future, we hope you will agree that this entertaining collection is one that will amuse and inspire the whole family.

Contents

Hugh Christie Technology College

Meadows School

Sevenoaks School

The Howard School

West Kent College

The Mini Sagas

Mostly Ghostly

I'm dreading it. The day has come, Uncle Bill is taking me for a ghost walk. I mean, I know it's not real but I hate ghosts and well, I know I'm going to see one.
We are walking down the old, dark lane and I feel scared but ... *Argh!*

Ella Proctor (12)
Combe Bank School

1

Emerald Eyes

Bella stepped into the gloomy corridor. It was so black she could not see anything! She peered into the darkness and saw two emerald eyes staring at her. They moved towards her. Bella was terrified. She struck a match and there, in the glow of the flame, was a kitten!

Abby McGowan (11)
Combe Bank School

Liger

She's a lion and a tiger. Her glorious stripes across her fur. Her purr is the sign of a lion. Her colour, it's the tiger side of her. She grew up in Africa, now she's in London Zoo. She's the most famous African animal - and the rarest. She's the liger.

Natasha Hawksworth (12)

Combe Bank School

3

Moody Horse

Lesson time, great. Who will it be this time? Aww, don't pull my saddle that hard! OK, she's on … Don't kick me that hard! OK, be cool … Look how high that jump is but oh, I'm in the air! That was fun but I'm still gonna buck her off …

India Welsh (13)
Combe Bank School

The Canal Path

Diane bought a gun. She was plodding along the canal path when a man came up behind her. He grabbed her by the cuff of her blouse and spun her round. He had a gun in his hand. Diane didn't know what to say. Then he said, 'You dropped this.'

Verity Sayer-Hitch (12)
Combe Bank School

A Surprise From Above

Something rustled behind him. He immediately
drew his sword from its sheath and started pacing
around in a circle. He looked up, and sitting in
a tree on the topmost branch was a beautiful,
young maiden with pearl-drop eyelashes. He
gazed at her in a daze of her beauty.

Libby Matthews (13)
Combe Bank School

A Day In The Life Of A Cat

A day in the life of a cat is very frustrating. Trying to catch my prey before it runs away. Sitting on the sofa relaxing peacefully, and then comes a human and pushes me right off. People treat me like a toy. Hugging me, kissing me, all day long.

Georgina Farrell (12)
Combe Bank School

7

The Teacher

I heard the click of his old Italian shoes coming
towards me, his narrow, brown, small eyes
looking at me and only me. I knew I had done
something but … 'You!' he angrily shouted. His
nose pointed straight at me, sharply.

'Yes, Sir, yes.'

'Go and get the register then!'

Daisy Kinghorn (12)
Combe Bank School

Dead Night

It was a cold winter night, snow falling faster by
the minute; James trudging through the snow.
When something clicked again and again, he tried
sprinting for the gate, but it was nowhere to
be seen. The wind howling hard like a banshee,
James fell face first into the snow.

Tori Morris (12)
Combe Bank School

9

Lost

Wandering slowly, heading home. Turn left into Fifth Street, or was it right into Second Street? So panic-stricken, I run every which way. An eerie breeze crawls down my neck. I turn a corner and there I am … or not! My heart is pounding, the fear astounding. *Argh!* Lost.

Lillian Dalton (13)

Combe Bank School

Sinister Shadow

A shark emerges from the cave. A big shadow
covers the whole shark and the whole cave.
There's an animal bigger and more sinister-
looking. The shark swims right up to the shadow.
The shadow slowly opens. The shadow closes
up. The sinister shark is trapped inside a sinister
whale.

Daisy Radwan (12)
Combe Bank School

11

The Elephant's Hats

There was an elephant with very big ears, so big he couldn't get his hats on. The elephant loved his hats and tried to wear one every day. He has lots of hats; spotty, stripy and curly. But the sad thing is, he can never wear them on his head.

Annabel Burnham (12)

Combe Bank School

Ella's Dangerous Moment

Ella stood on a branch. It creaked so loudly that
Ella screamed, destroying the freakish silence.
Becky laughed as she watched her friend attempt
to cross the river over the old, rotting branch. It
would've helped if Ella wasn't the sort of girl who
got easily frightened. But she was.

Becky Goddard (12)
Combe Bank School

13

The Dusty Ghost

I climbed down the ladder of the hole leading underground. I looked around. It was a dark room, cold and dusty. Suddenly the door of the hole slammed shut and a whirl of dust flew into my eyes. I could just make out a figure in the dust …

May Teverson (12)
Combe Bank School

A Day In The Life Of A Zebra

I'm running up and over the hills, away from the
lion. We must look like a lovely meal to him.
He's gaining speed on our herd, and I am not.
His mouth is open and *snap!* He hits a tree and
retreats. We have victory for the zebras! Yay!
Yippee!

Jessica Cooling (11)

Combe Bank School

15

Toys

Toys are boring, they don't do anything for
themselves. I mean, what's the point of having
a dead, stuffed lion when you could have a real
one? I could be traipsing through the jungle, ruling
everyone around. But now I come to think of it,
I'm lonely in my bed.

Susannah Kitto (11)
Combe Bank School

The Chase

I ran through the narrow hall, sensing their silent footsteps still pursuing me. I knew I was faster than them but I couldn't run forever! I could hear their heavy breathing, they were catching up. I would not give up, not to them, not when there were others at risk.

Anna Smith (12)

Combe Bank School

An Ant Called Bob

'Ouch! Not again. Why me? There are plenty
of other ants around.' Bob is an ant and a very
grumpy one too. It's only because he keeps being
stepped on. 'Why? Why?' he mumbles, annoyed.
None of his friends get stepped on. '*Ouch! Not
again!*' he sighs. 'It's sooo unfair!'

Jasmine O'Callaghan (11)
Combe Bank School

The Horror

She ran much deeper into the forest, scared of what was chasing her. The black figure was bigger than a horse. Suddenly the girl tripped on a twig. The black figure was coming closer. It was getting dark. Would she get away? The shadow faded and a mouse came out.

Jessie Cant (11)
Combe Bank School

The Abandoned

The creaks from the floorboards filled my ears.
The room felt lifeless, not a movement in sight. A
gush of air swept across me. It grew strong and
powerful. I challenged my way in the deserted,
gloomy room, against the rough winds that filled
the air with mysteriousness and dullness.

Sacha D'Arcy (11)
Combe Bank School

The End Of Humpty Dumpty!

Humpty Dumpty stood on the wall. Humpty Dumpty had a huge fall. All the king's horses and men couldn't be bothered to fix him together again. So they called Goldilocks and Little Red, but they were in bed. Then they saw Little Bo Peep walking by, but Humpty was *dead!*

Imogen Cox (11)
Combe Bank School

Two Pence Each

Once there was a boy who always stared through the steamy glass window. It smelled delicious, the crispy brown sausages all in a neat line on a shelf. He walked past the butchers after school and wanted to eat every one. 'How much are they each?'

'Two pence each, son.'

Millisa Dolke (11)

Combe Bank School

The Fox, The Rabbit And The Horse

I saw it. I saw the fox. It was there in my house.
It wasn't a normal fox though. It had a tail like
a horse and ears like a rabbit. I stared at it in
disbelief. I found out it was a cross between a
horse and a rabbit.

Jodie Williams (11)

Combe Bank School

23

Jeff, The Dog

Bang! What's that? A cat! Now it's on my mum's
flower bed. I have to get rid of it. I know, I'll bark,
then maybe Mum will let me out.
'Woof!'
She's here, the door's opening.
'Woof!'
Cat's gone, think I'll go back to bed.

Maddy Dadson (11)
Combe Bank School

Fishing And Dogs Don't Go

'Spot, come back!' screamed Emily as her dog
jumped into the river.
'Hey!' roared a man fishing. 'You scared away all
my fish!'
Terrified, Emily whispered, 'Spot.' Panting, Spot
emerged. Emily heard a noise. She turned around,
it was the man. Scared, she ran.

Olivia Theobald (11)
Combe Bank School

25

The Haunted Mansion

Up the creaky stairs I crept, around the trapdoor, the cold air blowing fiercely. I could see the shadow of the vampire. The door screeched open. I fell to the floor with horror. I felt the pain down my neck. I screamed with pain. I went blue. *'Argh!'*

Rebecca Mills (11)
Combe Bank School

A Friend For Sally

Alone on the streets, Sally felt cold and hungry. She had recently escaped from her violent stepfather, so she was so lonely. Suddenly she heard a whimper. Sally lifted a dirty box and there was a little puppy with beautiful eyes. 'Come here, I'll take care of you!' she said.

Eloise Phillips (11)
Combe Bank School

The New Neighbour

'What's that place?' asked Luke's new neighbour.
'That is the Thames Innovation Centre … Well it
used to be,' Luke replied.
'When did it shut down?'
'Supposedly when someone was murdered in
room 29.'
'Let's go in there!' exclaimed the new neighbour.
'Don't!' yelled Luke. But it was too late.

Holly Henderson (11)
Combe Bank School

Hazel, Not A Nut

Tears dripped from her face. Hazel had been humiliated in front of the whole class again. The texting queen won once more.
Will this last for long? Will Hazel's dad's advice finally help? Their school trip's coming up. Can Hazel stand being away from her family, or will she retaliate?

Georgia Spiteri
Combe Bank School

29

Untitled

A flash of red, then she bit me. I could feel pain,
excruciating pain. Writhing in agony, bloodcurdling
screams; that was me. My screams, my pain. A
menacing snigger. I was begging her to kill me, but
she left. Then death washed over me. Greeting
me. 'Jacob!' someone cried.

Hannah Thomas (13)
Combe Bank School

Untitled

Fineness of the dusk as it slipped from article to article to secrete itself. Hushing every noise until it was finally looming over the resting figure on the bed. Reaching over its shoulder, the silhouette retrieved sand, sprinkled it over the slumbering figure's eyes. The Sand Man slunk away.

Olivia Johnson (14)

Combe Bank School

A Day In The Life Of Granny Puckett

It was a dark, stormy night. Old Granny Puckett
was done. *Creak,* the rocking chair whined.
Granny sat thinking about her deceased husband
and the good times they had shared. Suddenly a
knock at the door interrupted her thoughts. She
opened the door.
'Trick or treat!' the little girl cried!

Jessica Goldsmith (13)
Combe Bank School

In The Life Of A Glamour Puss

Miss Princess Rapunzel her name is, with her long
golden hair. The prince called out, 'Let out your
hair,' so she did and the prince climbed up. But
… when he got there she was gone. The hair was
just a fake, cheap wig from ASDA.
'Sucker!' she called from below.

Francesca Redican-Clarke (12)
Combe Bank School

Not Such A Merry Christmas

The lit-up tree entranced me with its delicate glass decorations and perfectly hung tinsel. The presents placed neatly under the tree caught my eye. I leant out to pick one up, only to see my hand go through, leaving me clutching air once again.

Charlotte Swinglehurst (13)
Combe Bank School

34

Deception

It was not a normal day in Kent. This was the day I met my best cyber friend, Louise. Meeting the girl who comforted me and made me laugh every day meant everything to me, but Louise wasn't who I thought 'he' was …

Lucy Hart-MacNab (12)
Combe Bank School

Poor Prince Charming

My supposed Prince Charming galloped down
the cobbled drive once again. He dismounted and
called for me to come outside. I really didn't see
his problem. What was it that he saw in me? It's
as if he stalked me! So I shot the dirty blighter!
Phew, he was gone!

Camilla Pearson (13)
Combe Bank School

A Ghostly Going On

The creaky door opened. The screech of souls
scared the young boy, Joey, who saw a dead
body in the wooden door. Letters flowed out
everywhere spelling 'Be warned, don't go in
there'. He found no end …
Great story, but this story has no end. It's true!

Robyn Jones (13)
Combe Bank School

37

Murder In The Mansion

'I'll just be a second!' shouted Mrs Diblerry,
descending the grand staircase. 'Peter!' But a
deathly shadow lurked behind her.
Later the maid shouted, 'Mrs Diblerry's dead!'
But who did it? The maid, the butler or the cook?
Little did they know it was much closer
to home …

Rhiannon Doyle (13)
Combe Bank School

38

Should Have Listened

Walking swiftly through the woods with a bag of goodies from my visit with Gran, with a warm coat on. Suddenly a big, hairy wolf demanded my cakes. I explained to the wolf that they were out of date, but he ate them then died of food poisoning.

Annabelle Winter (12)
Combe Bank School

39

The Surprise Arrival

It was a dark, stormy night. Suddenly I heard footsteps coming towards me from behind the wooden door that creaked as the wind blew. I tiptoed to the old, cracked door. The footsteps came closer. The door opened. My father, he had come back, back from the war.

Natalie Tooze (13)
Combe Bank School

Santa, Is It You?

I could hear heavy footsteps behind me. Could it be Santa? Would it be Santa? Should I dare look behind me? The suspense was killing me. Just a peek wouldn't hurt. Taking my chance, I took a trembling breath and spun around. 'Dad, what are you doing here?'

Kaya Chew (12)
Combe Bank School

41

One Day My Prince Will Come

The young handsome prince strolled over to the beautiful girl lying in the glass case, guarded by seven dwarves. Opening the glass door he reached to kiss her. Suddenly Grumpy stormed over and grabbed the prince's coat. Grumpily he yelled, 'What are you doing? She's my wife!'

Amber Goodwin-Rose (13)

Combe Bank School

Take 2

Max plummeted from the 20th floor window.
He'd been pushed. His heart in his mouth as the
ground opened up, welcoming him to his coffin.
'This is it!' he screamed. He dared not look up at
his killer. *Crash,* he sank into the ground.
'Cut!' cried the director. 'Marvellous show!'

Alice Tarbert
Combe Bank School

The Race

Overwhelmed as I sprinted towards the finish.
'Yes!' I screamed. I had done it! The others were
miles behind. I had done it, I'd come first!
I made my way to the podium and …
'Come on, Louise, get out of bed. The race starts
in an hour!'

Rachel Hill (12)
Combe Bank School

Surprise, Surprise

Her cold, deep breath tickled the back of my neck as we wandered mindlessly down the dark, dusty steps of Greggory Castle. I could tell that she was very frightened. Slowly I turned the golden door handle and pushed it slightly open. 'Surprise, surprise!' yelled her family happily, 'Happy birthday.'

Katie Wardrop
Combe Bank School

45

Snow Pan

Gliding through the candyfloss clouds, Mr Peter
Pan, en route to see his darling Snow. It was her
final flying session. 'If you believe in yourself, you'll
fly,' said Peter.
She banished her nerves and dived at the window,
flapping her arms madly. 'I can fly … *ouch!*'

Lottie Shapland (12)
Combe Bank School

Fairy Glow

Jodi's eyes darted to the enormous tree planted in the enchanted forest. Millions of tiny fairies were crowding around, glowing vividly and illuminating their surroundings with a chromatic blaze. A sudden chill crept through the forest and the air produced a deafening *bang*, sending the fairies scattering away with fright.

Sophia Martin (12)
Dover Grammar School for Girls

The Ghost In The Village

One day in a small village there lived an old lady. The old lady had died many years ago, but her ghost still haunts the village today. The ghost does the lady's everyday chores, but every now and again the ghost does some mysterious things like killing people.

Hannah Lonergan (13)

Dover Grammar School for Girls

A Dog Named Bill

One day a dog named Bill went to Tesco and he
went on a purple bus. He saw an orange cat.
He bought two eggs, four carrots, cheese and
a Christmas tree. He then went to Iceland and
bought Christmas pudding. He then got on the
bus and went home.

Megan Baldwin (13)
Dover Grammar School for Girls

49

Untitled

The little, talented wizard removed his soft,
delicate hand from his magical box and pulled out
a magnificent blue and gold wand. The wizard
looked anxious, as if he were to do something
wrong, and then it happened. He shook his wand
vigorously and made the world change forever.

Danni Foster (14)
Dover Grammar School for Girls

What Happens Next?

Walking up the creaky black stairs, occasionally turning around making sure nothing was there, terrified of what could jump out, I continued. I reached the bedroom. Shaking, I opened the door. The smell was vile! Like something just died, or someone. The door slammed shut and I was trapped …

Chloe Allison (13)
Dover Grammar School for Girls

I Want My Daddy Back

Sometimes I wish Grandad was here again,
then Daddy wouldn't be so mad. Daddy would
stop hitting me. He would stop hurting me and
breaking me. I wish that Daddy wouldn't hit
Mummy. I wish for a lot of things, but most of all,
I wish for my daddy back.

Catherine Ashley (13)
Dover Grammar School for Girls

If Only ...

'No, stop. Please leave me alone!' cried a terrified, familiar voice. I recognised the meek voice coming from the distance. It was Eleanor's. As I pounded through the dark, gloomy wood, I suddenly came to a halt. Stabs in her neck, blood oozing from her ear, my pounding heart sank.

Katie Skelton (13)

Dover Grammar School for Girls

53

The 40-Year-Old Christmas Tree

Another Christmas and the tree is forty-four
years. The children wait nervously as Mum
assembles it.
'Christmas just won't be the same without
it,' Mum sighs. As Mum gets the last branch,
everyone holds their breath. Success! On goes
the star and the Christmas tree stands for another
year!

Beth Rayfield (14)
Dover Grammar School for Girls

The Escape

I ran and ran and ran, desperate to get away. I
needed to! However, I couldn't escape. The space
between me and my destination seemed miles.
I was never going to escape and be safe. Then I
realised, I was on a running machine.

Grace Findlay (13)
Dover Grammar School for Girls

The Shadow In The Alley

He was walking down the alley in pitch-black,
when he turned to look behind. There was a
shadow in the light at the end of the alley; the
shadow of a man with a knife. He started to run,
but the shadow was too fast …

Amy Brown (13)
Dover Grammar School for Girls

The Creature In The Sea

We walked slowly down the cold, frosty beach.
The waves lapped against the wall. All of a
sudden, we froze. I looked where he was pointing
and screamed in horror. We ran as fast as we
could, but it was faster. We stopped running and
held each other close.

Eden Winthrop (13)
Dover Grammar School for Girls

57

Haunting Voice

It was pitch-black as I felt my way along the corridor. Behind, floorboards were creaking and there were faint footsteps. Suddenly there was a bloodcurdling scream and I realised I was not alone … I tried fleeing - too late.
'You shouldn't be here,' I heard an eerie voice chant.

Lauren Kirkham (13)
Dover Grammar School for Girls

The Fright In The Night

Hastily I ran through the forest, lost and confused.
It was getting darker, the owls were screeching
into the night. A hand shot out, grabbing my arm.
I screamed, kicking violently, struggling to break
free. In my daze I heard a calm voice speaking to
me. It was only Dad!

Elizabeth Wright (11)
Dover Grammar School for Girls

The Summit

I'd been climbing for hours on end to the summit of Mount Everest. I reluctantly pulled my ice axe out of the white mountain face that lay before me. I knew this was it; this was the moment that I had been waiting for. That magnificent view was breathtaking.

Kirstie Kushana Maddison (13)
Dover Grammar School for Girls

Elfie And Eating, The Elves

Elfie and Eating disliked veg. Their boss, Fanto, told them, 'Green is a horrible colour, you shouldn't eat veg.' A bright light was upon Elfie and Eating. It's Princess 5-A-Day! Their faces shone. She threw apples into their mouths. They were cursed! They never ate junk food again!

Laura Wilshaw (13)

Dover Grammar School for Girls

Colourful Surprise!

One day there was a colourful rainbow. The colourful colours coloured the clouds. There were splashes of colours: red colours, pink colours, yellow colours and lots more colours! Everyone loved the colourful colours and decided to have a colourful parade! Colourful characters came to it from all over the world!

Taylor Munday (12)
Dover Grammar School for Girls

The Deed

The sweat was dripping off my brow as I trudged forwards. I was shaking at the thought of the deed with which I was burdened. Imagining all the scarlet-red blood that would be spilt because of me. 'One fine, plump turkey, please!'
The deed was done.

Erin Wakefield (12)
Dover Grammar School for Girls

Tutti To Frutti

Whoosh!
'What was that?' asked Hansel.
'Look, the house has changed. It's made out of fruit!' replied Gretel.
'It can't be!' protested Hansel.
'No! The candy canes have changed to bananas!'
'It must be this new healthy eating scheme. No sugar for us kids, Hansel, we're expected to be healthy.'

Chloe Broomfield (14)
Dover Grammar School for Girls

The Irony Of Age

As I lay still, I think to myself, *my life is nearly over.*
But thinking back to my early days I realise, I *am
like a baby again!* At 98, I'm bald, have no teeth,
can't change myself, and drool a lot. I still have
youth in old age!

Kara Adams (13)
Dover Grammar School for Girls

Lost In The Game

He rode through the city, lights burning the
night sky. He watched cars fall behind as he sped
through darkness. He began to drown in his
thoughts of how he would turn the next corner,
or overtake the next car until …
'Kai! Get off your Xbox, it's dinner time!'

Karris Simmons (13)
Dover Grammar School for Girls

MC' Dead

Landing in 3 … 2 … 1. I'm finally here, watery
eyes staring straight at it. A bright gold 'M'. It
must be … *Heaven!* Walking straight to the light,
the smell's wonderful. On Mars there's is nothing
like it. I'm going to like it here.
Two weeks later this life form was dead.

Kelly Tonkin (13)
Dover Grammar School for Girls

Moon Cheese

Lunar Jim went to the moon for a scientific experiment. He stepped onto the surface. It felt squidgy. Jim picked up a bit of moon and tasted it. It tasted like cheese. He loved cheese. Jim ate the whole moon and fell into space.

Natalie Wood (13)

Dover Grammar School for Girls

The Life Of Brian (And Of Kevin)

Kevin was a chipmunk. He was obese and unhealthy. His doctor warned him being overweight was dangerous. Kevin changed. He ate healthily and gained 10 yeas of his life back. He had a healthy party to celebrate. His twin brother, Brian, didn't change his ways. He died at the party.

Kayleigh Steele (13)
Dover Grammar School for Girls

69

Bean Running

'Run, run, run, as fast as you can. You can't catch
me, I'm the runner bean man!'
Chasing him were three overweight children and
their obese parents. They couldn't catch him but
two healthy children saw him and netted him in
seconds. They ate him and grew big and strong.

Hannah Zimmer (13)
Dover Grammar School for Girls

The Million Dollar Well

Jack and Jill went up a hill to fetch a pail of water.
They brought some friends who tried the water
and loved it so much that they wanted to buy it
bottled. Jack and Jill made their millions and paid
others to fetch the water.

Abbi Gosling (13)
Dover Grammar School for Girls

71

Little Piggies

This little piggy ate strawberries, this little piggy
ate sweets. The first little piggy was a healthy little
piggy and the second little piggy was obese.

Harriet Newton (13)

Dover Grammar School for Girls

Snow White And The Deadly Hamburger

The evil stepmother was jealous and decided to give Snow White a poisonous hamburger, to put her into a coma. When the prince heard what had happened, he bought an exercise DVD and an apple. Snow White smelt the apple, woke up and started Pilates. They lived healthily ever after.

Merregan Brown (13)
Dover Grammar School for Girls

Cherry Pie

Little Red Riding Hood arrived at her grandma's.
'Why Grandma, what rotten teeth you have! You
need to eat more healthily and cut down on the
sweets. Luckily, in my basket I have nothing but
fresh fruit and sugar-free sweets.'
Grandma groaned, 'All the worse to eat you with.'

Eloise Simes (13)

Dover Grammar School for Girls

Sweet Incentive

Hansel and Gretel stared at the screen, horrified.
Two expanding children were scoffing sweets
from a gingerbread house. As Hansel and Gretel
watched, the children's faces morphed into
their own and they knew they were heading for
obesity. They built a fruit house and changed their
lives for the better.

Alexandra Walter (14)
Dover Grammar School for Girls

75

Untitled

On the moon lived a dish who was married to a spoon. Unfortunately they had only ever served fast food.

One day in the newspaper, the dish read about how carrots were fashionable, so she ran off with a carrot, but as we all know, broccoli is more sexy.

Mollie Letheren Smith (13)

Dover Grammar School for Girls

Beneath The Coral

The water was murky and green. Beneath the coral were the remains of what had once been a living thing. As she peered deeper, a slimy creature smashed against the glass, latching on with its mouth. It made her heart race. She would never clean the fish tank again.

Gaby Northcott (11)
Dover Grammar School for Girls

Fire!

Red, orange and yellow everywhere. It was so hot. I could hear beeping in the corner of the kitchen. Smoke filled the air. Suddenly Mum walked in and opened the window. 'That's the third time this week you've burnt your dinner!'

Emily Royston (11)

Dover Grammar School for Girls

The Hungry Dragon

Dragon loved eating people. Every day he stomped outside to find a tasty snack. The king sent his best knight to kill Dragon. But he hadn't the heart. He took Dragon to a nearby forest and showed him that woodpeckers were tastier. The kingdom was rid of noisy woodpeckers forever.

Sadie Milton (11)
Dover Grammar School for Girls

79

The Gun

His hands wrapped tightly around the gun.
He crept around, listening for footsteps. He
turned and saw the rusty door. Raising the gun
he shouted, 'Put your hands in the …' The shot
resounded through the still night … *bang!* People
came flocking out of the building rejoicing. 'The
enemy is dead!'

Francesca Steeples (12)
Dover Grammar School for Girls

Uncle John

I sat asleep in my mother's chair when a creak occurred. I shot up out of the chair and grabbed the baseball bat that my dad kept in the corner. I saw a masculine figure, but it wore my mother's elegant dress that imaginatively waved in the wind. 'Uncle John?'

Katie Groombridge (12)
Dover Grammar School for Girls

81

A Creak In The Night

I was in bed when I thought, *are there supernatural beings? Are they evil?* I was pondering this when I heard a loud creak. I sat up. 'It's nothing,' I told myself. My door slowly opened. A little voice sounded out, 'Play with me!' I realised it was my brother!

Rebecca Mercer (11)
Dover Grammar School for Girls

The Hungry Dinosaur

Crash! Bang! The terrifying dinosaur's foot hit the floor. He smelt his dinner in the distance. 'Is that my dinner?' he bellowed. He ran as fast as his little legs would carry him. He tapped on a mouse's shoulder. She turned around. 'Yes, my darling. It's beef stew tonight.'

Rosie Adams (12)
Dover Grammar School for Girls

83

Little Beast

I was alone in the woods. It was evening. I couldn't find my way. I heard footsteps coming closer so I hid behind a tree, as a huge shadow loomed. A baby fox appeared, the setting sun distorting its shadow. I walked towards it and found my way.

Eleanor West (11)

Dover Grammar School for Girls

Little Red Riding Hood

One day my mum told me to take some biscuits to my nan. I walked through the woods. Someone was stalking me. Was this the end of me? I turned. Something hideously wolf-like was looking at me hungrily. 'Oh, hi Nan!' I said, relieved.

Katrina Austin (11)

Dover Grammar School for Girls

Little Cindy Star

When the talent scout visited her school, Cindy did not even consider auditioning. All the cool, confident girls did. Cindy just sat outside, alone as usual, singing softly to herself. Suddenly a man banged the door open. He stopped dead as he heard her song. 'Finally!' he exclaimed. 'My star!'

Martha Ford (11)

Dover Grammar School for Girls

The Princess And The Sweet Tooth!

Once upon a time there was a beautiful but spoilt princess, who had a very sweet tooth. She ordered her servants to bring her all the sweets in the kingdom. She sat eating every single sweet in sight. When she was finished, her teeth dropped out and her smile vanished.

Vicky Quinn (11)
Dover Grammar School for Girls

The Ride Of Her Life

Cling, clang, cling, clang! The girl's blood drained from her head, her tanned face went pale and her scream could be heard miles away. The roller coaster crawled to a halt; she stepped off. 'Could we go again?' the girl asked, her throat croaky from her screeches.

Holly Whitworth (11)
Dover Grammar School for Girls

88

Gulp!

Its smell was revolting. I could feel it tickling the tip of my tongue. I shut my eyes as tight as they would go. *Gulp.* I swallowed the Brussels sprout.

Amber Wright (12)

Dover Grammar School for Girls

89

The Theatre

Clap! Clap! Clap! The audience's hands clasped together all night long. Sitting in the old chair in the old grand circle, now used as a dressing room, I watched the performance of 'Romeo and Juliet'. Finally the curtains closed and I got up and left the dressing room, feeling tired.

Emelia Williams (11)

Dover Grammar School for Girls

The Wizard's Spell!

The seas began to crash and the skies began to
thunder as the wizards began to cast their spells.
It wasn't working, the opposite was happening.
Summer wasn't arriving as planned, it was leaving.
Winter was here instead. The wizards looked at
each other in despair. What had they done?

Megan Deary (11)
Dover Grammar School for Girls

91

What Is It?

It watched me carefully. Something was dripping
from the ceiling; slime or worse. The cave was
black as night. The beast was breathing heavily,
calmly, slowly. Trembling all around, my legs
turned to jelly. Slowly I snatched my silver, sharp
sword. The cold trickled down my spine. Sword
ready! Charge!

Bryony Ritchie (12)
Dover Grammar School for Girls

It Wasn't My Fault

Amy walked up to the house guarded by police.
She walked up the stairs to the bathroom. With a
tearful eye she looked at the blood-filled sink and
the white chalk outline of her sister, and she had
to tell herself it wasn't her fault ... when it was.

Abigail Taylor (11)
Dover Grammar School for Girls

The Thing From Behind The Bush

As I stared at the rustling, short bush, wondering what could be causing this mysterious, disturbing noise, there was a fierce burp which shook the park. Then out stomped a fish-breathed, chipped-toothed, full of hatred, ugly and battered sea creature. Trying, I guessed, to find its way home.

Emily Evans (11)
Dover Grammar School for Girls

Humpty Dumpty, The Story

Humpty Dumpty was sitting on the wall. He
leant back and fell off. The ambulance was called.
Humpty went to hospital and was mended.
The next day he had a visitor and he was all
excited. He fell out of bed and he could not be
put back together again.

Marina Robinson (11)
Dover Grammar School for Girls

Just Sing A Lullaby

Every night I always hear the delicate fairies in
the garden. When I look through my curtains,
I see them dancing in the glistening moonlight
among the flower pots, singing amongst the
amethyst flowers and playing a wonderful tune on
their instruments, which sends me drifting into a
dreamless sleep.

Stacey Marshall (13)
Dover Grammar School for Girls

The Topaz Orb

I slumped onto the dewy grass, closing my eyes dazedly. Suddenly a topaz sparkle shimmered around my splayed hands. It glistened beautifully in the silver moonlight. I stretched my curious arm out to touch the twinkling, diamond-like orb, but a pearly dragonfly stared back and hovered away.

Nicola Dunsbee (12)

Dover Grammar School for Girls

Faerie King

Squelch.
'Ugh!' My gossamer-stockinged foot sank into
yet another squalid puddle. The faeries of
Queen Titania's court would not be amused,
but she would be incandescent. I tiptoed in
sheepishly, my iridescent wings soaked and my
gorgeous, hideously impractical gown practically
disintegrating. 'How dare … ? Oh, it's you,
Oberon.'

Josephine Carter (12)
Dover Grammar School for Girls

Long Summer Sun

Lizzy was a young fairy. She met a vampire on a long summer's evening. Little did she know that Grayham was a vampire. They kissed under the sunset, until one day he bit her. The venom passed through her body. Lizzy and Grayham were never seen again.

Ellie Pile (12)
Dover Grammar School for Girls

Traitor?

She's mischievous, cunning and stunningly
beautiful. This fairy's mood swings can make her
do the craziest things, good and bad.
One time she became a traitor to the kingdom.
What had she done? Her conscience was bugging
her! She couldn't take it. She needed to get the
records straight.

Marie April Wiggins (12)
Dover Grammar School for Girls

The Lights

'Go away!' Sparkling lights danced around my head. I flapped my hands to usher them away. Giggling like church bells floated through the air. Minuscule hands pulled at my shirt. I caught a glimpse of delicately embroidered clothing as the lights floated away. It was those Blackmoore Wood faeries again.

Shelbie Adams (12)
Dover Grammar School for Girls

The Fairy Child

A young girl of a fairy and human was blessed
and loved. She was the prettiest fairy of the fairy
world. Her friends were jealous so instructed
the crazy old man to kidnap Pop. He put her in a
tower.
One day John freed her. They married on a hill.

Sophie Stevenson (13)
Dover Grammar School for Girls

The Silhouette

The silhouette danced in the stray sunbeam that broke through the jaded forest. Mesmerising, piercing eyes stared out, their background a tiny, perfect, porcelain face. Delicate wings fluttered elegantly, illuminating the shadows beyond. A complex of silver hair sat upon her head. Hypnotic … but she had disappeared, gone for eternity.

Sharna Bevan (13)
Dover Grammar School for Girls

Fairies Aren't Always Perfect!

Suddenly a stroke of mist appeared over the rainbow and there, floating in mid-air, were two fairies. They were just as I thought they would be: brown hair, pink clothes and glitter-covered wings. But no, there were two fairies fighting over the pot of gold. How lovely?

Hannah Carruthers (12)

Dover Grammar School for Girls

Help!

She walked through the door and *bang,* the fairy trap that we had set the day before had gone off. We ran and there she was, in a heap on the floor …
She's dead. The fairy queen is dead! This is all our fault. What are we going to do?

Tara Lawless (12)
Dover Grammar School for Girls

Tink And Pete

Dark, shiny hair glistening in the moonlight.
Purple, stunning dress with big, beautiful wings
bursting out of it. As she flew, her hair was
whistling in the wind. Racing to her destination,
Tinkerbell saved Peter by eating the cake.
A little girl was watching 'Peter Pan' at her house.

Ellie Pepper
Dover Grammar School for Girls

What Is It?

It is a dark, gloomy night! I see a light … what is
it? Out comes the most amazing, magnificent fairy
ever. The blue dress, with the glistening silver
tiara nestling on her shimmering blonde locks. I
think it's a fairy? *Bang!* She's gone, nowhere to be
seen. Gone forever?

Jessica Butcher (12)
Dover Grammar School for Girls

The Shadow!

Atlantis, the garden fairy, appeared. She was asked to go into town to pick up some flowers for the party.

A few hours passed and Atlantis did not arrive. The other fairies began to worry. Suddenly a dark shadow cast upon Pennsylvania. No one was found, apart from Atlantis' ghost.

Chloe Allman (13)

Dover Grammar School for Girls

Peter Pot And Tinkerwell

There was a boy called Peter Pot. He never
wanted to grow up.
'Tinkerwell, where are you? There you are!'
They went to Neverland, then got stopped by
Captain Crook. They couldn't escape. There was
no one to help them. Was this the end for Peter
and Tinkerwell?

Rhian Stone (12)
Dover Grammar School for Girls

Big Sloppy Kiss!

'Argh!' cried Sleeping Beauty. When she was asleep she was dreaming about a prince waking her with a kiss but … instead she woke up with a *big, ugly, wicked frog.* He didn't seem to mind kissing. He gave her a big sloppy kiss and said he wanted to marry her.

Nicole Savage (12)
Dover Grammar School for Girls

Peer Pressure

These flawless moonbeams jeer at this self-despising tree, and poison these rivers which loathe the reflection. Envious is the tree of these luminous rays. Quick glints of lightning engrave these crevices into this tortured bark. Unsatisfying pain, but these scars run deep along these limbs. Relentlessly these rivers flow.

Lauren Hollowday (14)
Dover Grammar School for Girls

Untitled

First a smooth calm sphere of life sitting under a
blanket of soft protective feathers. A small crack
appears on the surface. Crack turns into hole until
there is a flash of yellow. After a long, challenging
fight for freedom, the duckling pokes his head out
into the shining sunlight.

Katherine Vance (14)

Dover Grammar School for Girls

The Monster In The Lake

I ran from the guards. I heard them yelling as I dived into the river. I swam with all my might, desperate to get miles away. Then … a soul-shaking moan. It came from a repulsive beast grabbing my foot. I had no more oxygen. 'Dad! *Let go!*' I spluttered.

Rhiannon White (14)
Dover Grammar School for Girls

The House

The frost gripped his soul. He edged further towards it with trepidation. The moon magnified the eeriness of the shack. He heard the scream of an innocent woman. He was intrigued by the secrets that lay behind the door. He was snatched suddenly, his story ending there with the others.

Shannon Clark (15)

Dover Grammar School for Girls

Survival

My lungs burned for air. I raced through the empty corridors, intent on escaping from them. Footsteps sounded in my ears and the smooth grey stone of the walls blurred in motion. I darted round a corner and stopped suddenly. Waves of despair washed through me. I was not alone.

Lizzie Grilli (14)
Dover Grammar School for Girls

After Band On Monday

Band finished. The playground was pitch-black.
The only lights to be seen were those in the main
buildings, but those were miles away.
I must run to cover the vast stretch of tarmac
before they get me. The bright lights get clearer
and clearer, till I'm safe at last.

Siân Robinson (15)
Dover Grammar School for Girls

Bright Eyes

He woke with a start, his breathing frantic. He could hear a noise. A growling noise, growing louder, louder. His panicked heart momentarily froze as he met the glare of two evil, penetrating eyes. Frenzied, trembling with fear, he fumbled for the light - only to find it was the cat.

Charlotte Davies (14)

Dover Grammar School for Girls

Traveller

I stepped out of the cab, met by lights gleaming against the night sky. It had been an extensive journey from my small Texan town, but finally I had arrived. The instantaneous hustle and bustle primarily confused me, but I was quickly distracted - distracted by the wonder that's New York.

Ruth Bailey (15)
Dover Grammar School for Girls

Lifeless Walking

Each step towards home made them resurface.
I thought at least maybe that death would
release me from this heartbreaking pain and the
memories, or maybe that death would be worse
than life itself. I realised long ago that I had no final
destination, but my broken feet trudged onwards.

Sarah Buchanan (14)
Dover Grammar School for Girls

The Chase

I could hear their ragged breathing behind me as they followed me into the woods. Their footsteps didn't even falter. My lungs burned with exertion and my legs ached as I forced them forwards. I couldn't stop. The warm bundle in my arms demanded that I go further and faster.

Jessica Finch (14)
Dover Grammar School for Girls

Darkness

Cold, desolate darkness surrounds me. I look
around with wide eyes, shaking with fear.
Suddenly a loud growl fills the room. I freeze. I
breathe faster as footsteps approach. I bite back a
scream as lifeless hands grab me by the shoulders.
With no warning, I fall and all disappears …

Rowan Adams (14)
Dover Grammar School for Girls

Running Through The Woods

There was nothing there, just the mischievous shadows. Relief rushed over me as I sank back on a tree. Suddenly I felt the tree twitch. I spun round to find that what I was leaning on wasn't a tree but the monster, grinning back at me, eyes ablaze with victory.

Lauren Macmillan (15)
Dover Grammar School for Girls

Sorry

I flinched as his fingers sketched the outline of the gash that curved down my cheek. The memories were as bittersweet as the blood in my mouth: his bear-like frame towering over me, smashed bottle grasped in his palm. 'Never again,' he murmured. 'I'm sorry petal.'
Sorry? Liar, liar.

Katharine Wiggell (14)
Dover Grammar School for Girls

123

Diving Lessons

I shuffled to the edge. My whole body trembled with fear. I hesitantly peered into the shimmering surface below me. I stretched my arms up and bent my knees. I took one last look and jumped. I plummeted towards the water. *Splash!* I've finally learnt to dive in the pool!

Charlotte Miles (14)

Dover Grammar School for Girls

Could You Imagine?

She stared into my eyes, focusing, whispering,
'Fairies.' That's it! One simple word. *Fairies*, I
repeated it in my head. She leant back smiling.
'They're real, you know,' and lying in her cupped
hands was a glowing figure. I believed her then.
Suddenly a little chiming voice, 'Hello.'
Wow! Fairies!

Grace Cobbold (12)
Dover Grammar School for Girls

125

The Impatient Beast

Lucy said goodbye. The monster let out a mighty roar and inched forward, quite obviously getting impatient. Its eyes brightened as Lucy prepared herself for what was to come. Lucy's mum braced herself and drove away from the friendly household in their brand new car.

Alice Wyatt (13)
Dover Grammar School for Girls

The Lonely Dream

I ran, breathing heavily, pleading to the god to let me live. I heard the loud footsteps and breathing. I ran. I fell hard and screamed. I felt something tug at my leg, my hair, and then something pulled at my arms. I was being dragged!
Then I woke …

Talya Moxom (12)
Hugh Christie Technology College

The New Island

As I take my first step, I feel the mad wind blow
at me, covering me with mist. The bushes rustle.
I see the tribal men with spears and bows. They
run for me. I run from them, but they catch
me ...

Ayden Kenway (12)
Hugh Christie Technology College

When I Was A Fish

Diving, swimming and gliding through the freezing
water, as my scales glisten through the waves.
Suddenly, a gigantic black and fearsome whale
speeds after me! I quickly swim from side to side,
not looking where I am going. Finally I look up; A
shadow emerges from the distance … *Bang!*

Jake Regan (12)
Hugh Christie Technology College

The Fury Of The Sea

Swipe! The shark was aggravating the declining shoal of fish; the fish frantically darting away. the shark, now in need of desperate satisfaction of its hunger. The declining shoal; they were in desperation of satisfaction of their great escape. *Snap,* as the shark enclosed the fish. The shark had won.

Daniel Veness (12)

Hugh Christie Technology College

The Creature

He was running, weaving in and out of people,
trying to get away. He jumped onto a roller
coaster and so did it. It was moving closer and
closer. He was getting more scared as it came
closer. A chill ran down his spine as the
creature …

Owen Marshall (12)
Hugh Christie Technology College

131

The Beast

The forest was dead, frozen in silence. The only sound I could hear was the crackling of the fire. My heart was beating faster and faster. I was terrified. I could hear it coming closer and closer. It was on a mission to destroy the forest, to kill me ...

Chloe Marchese (12)
Hugh Christie Technology College

In The Woods

A twig snapped. A shiver ran through the child as a bony hand gripped his frightened body. Rigid with fear, the child turned and saw a swollen, distorted face. The child ran blindly through the undergrowth, not stopping until he was safely home, praying he wasn't followed.

Charlie Williams (13)
Hugh Christie Technology College

133

Unlucky

He was limping, there was blood everywhere.
He had been attacked by a lion! He was trying to
hurry. He didn't want the pride coming back for
seconds. Too late, he collapsed and the pride had
found him. He was another meal for the lions.

Joshua Treharne (12)
Hugh Christie Technology College

Dangerous Water!

Smack! John's boat crashed into a gigantic rock. *Splash!* John bombed himself into the freezing water. Whilst swimming, something mysterious was lurking behind him. *A shark!* Suddenly he was swimming for survival. *Crunch!* Its jaws crunched down repeatedly on his fragile bones. He was now trapped and gone forever!

Ben Holder (13)

Hugh Christie Technology College

Apocalypse Comes True

The news had just come in. 'The end of the world!' they exclaimed. Everyone was packing. The electricity was fading fast. People dashing, the earth was cracking. There was a faint scream of excitement and fear in the background … 'Stop!' screamed Lizzy. 'Tilly, no!' But it was too late.

Katie Nettle (11)
Hugh Christie Technology College

The Ghost Bell

'Watch it!' screamed Max. Johnny leapt off the
rusted tower. 'Stop it!'
'What?' replied Johnny.
'You know what!'
'Well obviously I don't.'
'If I didn't do anything, well who did, 'the ghost
of this church?' said Max sarcastically. His phone
rang …
'Hello Max, I'm watching you, Max.'

Ryan Hoy (11)
Hugh Christie Technology College

137

The Ghostly Event

Suddenly a noise came from outside Pixie Hollow.
What was it? Now it was coming closer and
closer, the pixies were hiding under huge leaves
and in tiny squirrel holes. Then it was there, a tall
dark shadow with bright green eyes. It picked up
a pixie … *Oh no!*

Casey Spendiff (11)
Hugh Christie Technology College

Run

'Run!' screamed Mrs Baldwin to the pupils as she saw two red eyes in the bushes. Just then, Mr Palmer had vanished! After that they huddled together and thought, *what happened to him?* They flagged down a car and saw him being carried off by a shadowy figure …

Luke Smith (11)

Hugh Christie Technology College

Pixie Path

Tina and Maria were upstairs watching telly and
doing their nails. Their mum said, 'Go out, it's a
sunny day,' so they went out and had a walk and
found a path.
'Oh look, a path,' said Tina. 'Let's go and explore.'
What will they find?

Regan Norman (11)
Hugh Christie Technology College

The Cannibal

Screeching in the night. I looked outside, there was nothing there. Then I looked behind me and there was a knock at the door. It was a cannibal! I screamed but no one could hear. Next thing, my mum came home. I was lying there with no head.

Nicholas Parr (11)

Hugh Christie Technology College

What Is It?

I opened the cold wooden door, covered in wet
ivy, with care. It creaked all the way as I opened
it. As I walked through the door it slammed
and locked shut. Something cold touched my
shoulder. I screamed. No one could hear me. I
was forever trapped and forgotten.

Heather Wenn (12)
Hugh Christie Technology College

Wembley Cup Final

England and Brazil's game had ended in penalties. Brazil started. The people fell dead silent. Ronaldhino scored, the crowd went crazy. Beckham was next, and scored. Robinho was next in line. He ran towards the ball and smashed it home. Could England go on to win the World Cup?

Dean Barden (11)

Hugh Christie Technology College

Lava Mountain

Josh was clinging on for life. 'Oli, don't let go!' yelled Josh. Oli wasn't going to. Josh was Oli's best friend. But Josh was too heavy for Oli, he was slipping like he was on oil, and then someone grabbed them. It was Dan, but could he hold them? *Argh!*

Oliver Priestley (11)
Hugh Christie Technology College

A Day In The Life Of Nick

One day I went to school to see Jarath and Jack.
On the way I saw two red eyes in the bush. I
ran to school, I then told Jarath and Jack. They
laughed and said, 'You've got a good imagination,
Nick!' and walked off.
I was telling the truth!

Jarath Steadman (11)
Hugh Christie Technology College

Jungle Havoc

It had landed; a brilliant, glowing shed. Nick and Ben walked excitedly into the shed. There was a button. It was pressed. They landed. They wandered out in shock. It was a jungle. Suddenly something roared behind them. Something big, scaled, with big, sharp teeth and big, green eyes.

Clara Kelley (11)
Hugh Christie Technology College

A Quest Through Toadstool Temple

It was a dark, stormy night. Azalia and Alex were wandering through Toadstool Temple. This was the temple that they had discovered. Suddenly there was a loud noise coming from behind them. Azalia was excited and wanted to explore. Will they survive the quest?

Holly Wright (11)

Hugh Christie Technology College

The Swan's Luck

Hickory, dickory, dock, the swan swam up the loch. The swan got excited and very delighted as the fish was out of luck. He was completely and utterly stuck, so the swan got in there and swallowed him up!

Katelin Field (12)

Hugh Christie Technology College

Cut!

'Don't do it, Johnny!' screamed Sam. 'You can't do this! Have mercy! I didn't mean to hurt your family, it was an accident.'
Johnny laughed excitedly. He reloaded the gun, *bang!*
Sam cried endlessly.
'Cut, cut, cut. Well done. Very good. Take five!'
But was the actor really dead?

Bradley Page (12)
Hugh Christie Technology College

149

Tampered?

Everyone fell silent when the brake cable broke.
The Top Gear studio was shocked. Captain Slow
had smashed the wall! He had made the car shoot
forward in his excitement. Then came Gambon.
He tried to force the brakes to stop him from
crashing. Did someone tamper with them?

Ryan Reid (12)
Hugh Christie Technology College

The Loop

Clink, clank ... The car was dragged up the track
with the sight of speed appearing. Its time came
as it raced down the track at 100mph! The
ferocious loop was in slight but ... the wheel
came loose!
'No!' screamed the riders, but unheard as the car
clanked along the track ...

Connor Marchant (12)
Hugh Christie Technology College

151

The Presents

It was Christmas morning. Jack woke up, he leapt out of bed and sprinted downstairs. *Wow!* There were tonnes of fantastic, colourful presents. He was so excited. He stared at the Christmas tree, it sparkled as bright and pretty as a star. He couldn't wait to start opening the presents.

Joshua Hill (12)

Hugh Christie Technology College

The Cave Of Mystery

'Nearly there!' bellowed Mrs Baldwin so everyone on the coach could hear her. Although she shouted, her voice was overwhelmed by the excited chatters of 7SB! Suddenly the bus screeched to a halt, like an elephant catching sight of a mouse. 7SB had arrived at the mysterious cave.

Lauren Henderson (11)
Hugh Christie Technology College

Dad Went Up The Clock

Hickory, dickory, dock, Dad ran up the clock. The clock went *bang!* and Dad went *clang!* Hickory, dickory, dock.
The mouse ran up, Dad was down, then Dad ran up and the mouse was down. Then Dad fell down. Dad said, 'Ow!' and the mouse went, 'Wow!' Hickory, dickory, dock.

Jazmin Cole (11)
Hugh Christie Technology College

The Moment

The guns were blaring. The sergeant said to retreat. No one did. 'Keep going!' shouted Jefferson.
'Why?' I said. But there was no answer. I turned around. Tragically Jefferson was dead. All of a sudden, guns stopped. But why? No one knew. Everything stopped, then it all started over again.

Ciaran Shortland (11)
Hugh Christie Technology College

155

An Exciting Fairy Tale Story

In the extraordinary Pixie Palace, the tiny pixies
were dancing to the magnificent music. Suddenly
and enormous giant crushed the pixies.
The next day a beautiful golden unicorn came
cantering down and his horn touched the pixies
and healed them. 'Wow!' shouted the pixies in
surprise.
What will happen next?

Charlotte Yates (11)
Hugh Christie Technology College

West Ham Cup Final

West Ham are in the FA Cup Final. Drawing 3-3
with Tottenham, there are five minutes left. Scott
Parker's on the ball. He puts it over the top to
Franco. Woodgate tackles him. It's a penalty.
Dimanti hits it with *great* power. It hits the back
of the net!

Regan Corke (11)
Hugh Christie Technology College

Dino Dog

'Argh!' screamed Jim in terror. 'Leave me alone!'
he cried. The vicious dinosaur-like beast stepped
closer and Jim came to a dead end. He was
trapped!
Suddenly a huge voice from a giant was heard.
'Fido, be a good dog and leave that poor worm
alone.'

Oscar Collis (12)
Hugh Christie Technology College

Break In

'This door can't hold forever,' shouted a soldier. 'Keep trying,' replied General Scar, 'let nothing through!'

Just then the door blasted open, knocking them back. A dark knight walked through. Several beasts followed, killing the soldiers. Scar was being tortured by dark magic. Who was behind this?

Thomas Souter (11)
Hugh Christie Technology College

The Explorer And The Great Golden Stone

I travelled for many days and nights to get there, but when I did, he was there, laying there upon a rock which was the great golden stone. My quest was over. My hope was for nothing. The explorer beat me to this great golden stone. I had lost.

Alex Chauvin (12)

Hugh Christie Technology College

Myfly

The best roller coaster in the world is at Myfly, the new island. It's like going through the eye of a tornado, riding a mental, wild tiger. A boy was riding it once but he fell off into the ocean. However, he was saved by …

Matthew Wilson (12)
Hugh Christie Technology College

Somewhere Else

I was walking from school and was excited and sad because my pet had died and I was going to get a new pet. I was daydreaming and then when I was back to Earth, I noticed I was somewhere else. Somewhere magical! Then I noticed that everything talked!

Aimee Trebilco (12)

Hugh Christie Technology College

Bank Robbery

Today I went to the bank with my dad, and this monster of a man came in and took me hostage. Then the police burst in and they took me with them, and there was a huge chase. Then we clipped the back of the car and then … *bang!*

Jack Waghorn (12)
Hugh Christie Technology College

The House Of Doom

In the house of doom there is a magical bookshelf.
One book in the house will lead you to a haunted
hatch. Will this lead you to a way out, or lead you
to the end of life? The grandfather clock strikes
twelve. Will you choose life or death?

Luke O'Neil (11)
Hugh Christie Technology College

Assassination

The guards suddenly got pelted with arrows.
General Cassius quickly got on his horse and
rode off into the distance. He could see shadows
following him, his heart pounded. Suddenly he fell
to the ground with one arrow through his neck,
then he was silenced. Barbarians!

Ben Newman Hodge (12)
Hugh Christie Technology College

165

Tricked

I was playing in the garden, ran to get the ball
and saw a door in the tree. I went to open it.
A beautiful path was there. How did it appear?
Wasn't there before. An adventure! I was so
excited. Then this shadow swallowed me …

Lucy Souter (11)
Hugh Christie Technology College

Tragedy

'Today is the final of the F1 championship,' said the excited commentator. 'This is Silverstone. Lewis Hamilton has taken an early lead.' Now it's Jenson Button on the inside. Hamilton is spinning like a plane doing tricks. Hamilton is going into the barrier!' The crowd watched in excitement …

Craig Tooth (11)

Hugh Christie Technology College

A Day In The Life Of ...

His name was Tie. He was a huge monster with
tiny tusks and nearly-demolished feathers, and an
ugly face. He felt miserable. He woke at lunch,
ate ten toilets, then slept again.
Later, he woke and ate chocolate flapjack and
went back to sleep in the bath.

Nathan Blight (13)

Meadows School

I Was Terrified

I was marching down the road when a grown
man snatched me off my feet and dragged me to
his house and tortured me. I could not speak. I
was terrified! I cut the rope and I sprinted away.

Kobi Norman (13)

Meadows School

He's Not Alone

He went upstairs to a room. A room that was
haunted, a room that someone had died in. There
was a ghost that would kill you. A ghost that
would hunt you down then kill you!
So watch out, the ghost is following you!

Jordan Kettlety (13)
Meadows School

The Hunted

An innocent-looking duck was swimming across the murky, bubble-filled swamps happily, until it saw a ferocious-looking shark on the other side of the pool. It swam as fast as it could but the shark kept getting closer. Then a voice came from downstairs, 'Come down, dinner's ready!'

Shyam Kalairajah
Sevenoaks School

The Poker Match

The chips were stacked on the table. He put the chips in, all of them. No going back now. He took a sip of water from his transparent cup. Sweat rolled down his face, he looked very anxious. Billy stuck his hand in, grabbed all the chips and ate them.

Alex Newman (12)
Sevenoaks School

The Race

Warmth inside compels me to continue. I feel
totally alive.
'Allez!'
Race on. An erupting sound. I glance behind.
Death is chasing. The wave of snow is
approaching. I can't save myself. It's over now.
Tape connects with body. Voices chant my name.
I can breathe again. I am spared.

James Robson (12)
Sevenoaks School

What A Nice Grandma I Have!

That was close, Ruby thought to herself as she wandered slowly back to her gran's house. 'Gran!' Ruby screamed. 'The wolves nearly ate me!' 'Poor darling, you must be cold. Go sit by the oven to warm up. Tell me what happened,' Gran replied as she sharpened her carving knife.

Verity Thomson (12)
Sevenoaks School

Robin Hoodie

He rides around his council estate in a stolen
Vauxhall Corsa with a pin stripe, neon lights and
a spoiler. He walks around town with his Adidas
tracksuit around his ankles. He sells fake watches
and has a fake tan. He steals from the rich and
steals from the poor!

Alex Bridges (12)
Sevenoaks School

Let Me Pass

'Let me pass!' the girl said.
'Say the magic word.'
'You should not be rocking back on your chair
anyway.'
'You still cannot pass.'
'Let me through, *now!*'
'No, I wo …' exclaimed the boy as he toppled
backwards off his chair.
So the girl went round the other way!

Emma Kemp (13)
Sevenoaks School

Gingerbread And Smarties

One day Holly and Guy were out walking in the woods, when they came across a trail of breadcrumbs. They followed the crumbs and came across a house made of all things nice. They entered the house, almost hunting for the owner. Then they heard a noise from the oven …

Rebekah Collins (12)

Sevenoaks School

Forget What?

She left her house but forgot why. He would go
to the see-through wall, but forget to go back
home. She would meet him and then meet him.
He would wander the same path over and over.
They lived in a bowl, blowing bubbles, people
tapping on the glass.

Chloe Rouse (13)
Sevenoaks School

The Chase

The trigger's pulled, *bang!* I run and don't stop. I get tired and slow down, but the people behind me are gaining on me. I can't stop. Eventually I come to a dead end and have to stop. Suddenly someone comes behind me and says, 'You've won your 400m race!'

Chloe Broom (12)
Sevenoaks School

What Really Happened To Grandma

The wolf was standing in court, accused of the murder of an old woman. 'I did not eat that granny,' he pleaded, 'children are far more tasty.' Meanwhile, in the back of court stood a young girl in red, still picking her teeth, trying to cover up a small burp …

Guy Parfitt (13)
Sevenoaks School

The Haunted Classroom

The classroom was haunted; ghosts remained.
She looked around and froze. Her eyes followed
a trail. It led to a monster. She opened the door
and ran. Outside was a graveyard. She heard
the door and turned. The last sight she saw
was monsters and ghosts pouncing. She woke,
screaming.

Flora Cournane (12)
Sevenoaks School

The Hunted

Panic flashed across the fox's eyes. Shaking with fear, it raced through the trees. A stampede of hooves followed in heavy pursuit. The blur of red fled through every near field and wood until it could go no further. The nearest hunter grinned wickedly and raised his gun. *Bang!* Red.

Laura Lyttle (12)
Sevenoaks School

Extinct

'Mummy, what's this?' asked Sophie, staring at the figure in front of her. They were looking at the skeleton of a creature so tall, towering over them with long tusks and sturdy bones, powerful and tough.

'This amazing mammal was alive many years ago,' Mother replied. 'This is an elephant.'

Emma Harrington (12)
Sevenoaks School

The Disastrous School Plays

I wanted to be an angel; I was a Christmas pudding. I wanted to be a star; I was a wood chopper with a moustache. I wanted to be a wicked witch; I was a beggar playing my violin quietly in the background, so I was seen but not heard.

Molly Owen (12)
Sevenoaks School

Fate

I was always fated to be left behind. At birth, they confused me with another baby and I was left at the hospital.
As a child, I was left after school, waiting to be collected.
After my return from university, I discovered that my family had disappeared without a trace.

Amy Severs (12)
Sevenoaks School

Venturing In The Snow

Ten days till Christmas and the earth was blanketed in perfectly white snow. I ventured out; I wanted to find an adventure. I walked forward, oblivious to my actions and then realised what I was doing. No one knew where I was going, no one knew I was gone.

Catherine Stratton (12)

Sevenoaks School

A Game Of Tig

It stood there, staring, ready for the kill.
Sprinting, trying to avoid its touch, the feeling of
overwhelming adrenaline as I dodged through this
never-ending labyrinth. I plunged into darkness.
Spinning round relentlessly, I flew out. It was
standing there. It swiped me.
I now had to chase him.

James Hale (12)
Sevenoaks School

187

Lonely Tidings

I'm doomed to float around old Denton Manor.
My butler cannot see me, however much I
clamour. Now I don't need him. Needs are
from the past. Haunting is my job. It won't be
accomplished fast. Throughout the ages, I've
dreaded these times. Now there's consolation in
haunting these times.

James Bache (12)
Sevenoaks School

Hockey Match

Hearts pounding, we strap on our armour, our mouths dry. Though I sense danger, I cannot run away. I've worked too hard for this.

We march to the field; perfect, green. For a moment, although our faces are the same colour as milk, we are hopeful. Then the game begins …

Emma Gull (12)
Sevenoaks School

189

The Death Of Anne Boleyn

She was brought to the block. Her petite figure was steady. The executioner licked his lips, bracing himself. She then knelt upright, the French way. Her ornaments were removed and she was blindfolded. The executioner distracted her. 'Where is my sword?' And in one swift, clean stroke, she was gone.

Daya Srinivas (12)
Sevenoaks School

Knife Crime

He dawdled home from school, choosing a shortcut. The area's rough, but it was cold. He cut sharp into an alleyway. In the distance he sighted five silhouettes, but trudged on regardless, his eyes darting around. Suddenly a searing pain tore across him, then he was swallowed by an abyss.

Henry Bowers (12)
Sevenoaks School

Life And Death

Two are born; one into wealth and love, the other into poverty and hardship. A pampering mother to tend all needs, versus a sister barely old enough to care for herself. The poorer toils to make a better life, the richer enjoys the silver spoon. Life ends. All is equal.

Abigail Hands (12)
Sevenoaks School

An Orwellian Dictatorship

In the English countryside, a rebellion takes place.
The conquered fight back, but soon abandon their
case. New rules are established by which all must
abide. But the fighting continues, everyone takes
sides. Executions ensue; there are graves to dig. Is
it communism or a dictatorship? Just ask the pig.

Max Cunningham (12)
Sevenoaks School

193

Too Late

My beloved dog was always by my side. His glassy, glinting eyes zipped around like dragonflies. But one day, my precious pet wasn't there. The smell of car fumes tentatively attacked my nose. I stood motionless on the road looking at the mangled mess, still warm, next to my feet.

Rosemary Donald (12)
Sevenoaks School

Chase

Tyres squealed. I was off. My small car had hardly
any pace, but I was a touring car driver. As the
police caught up with me, my heart was almost
beating in time with their sirens. I clenched the
wheel tightly, swerved into the oncoming traffic.
A mighty crunch sounded ...

William Parr (12)

Sevenoaks School

The Story Of A Lifetime

My water world exploded. I was in my element: air. An upright citizen I became, independent. Adventures were mine. I created beings in my own image - well almost. Then, dependent once more was I, somehow less upright. Finally, quite horizontal. No longer familiar air but deep, dark earth enshrouded me.

Anna McGee (13)

Sevenoaks School

Control

Anger floods his body. He grabs her lifeless hand, twists it. The crunch as it rips from her socket pleases him. He bashes her against the ground, her delicate body slamming across the floor. Her eyes flicker and stare unseeingly. Power. A voice: 'What have you done to my doll?'

Olivia Brandon (12)
Sevenoaks School

HMSS Endeavoured

I'm travelling through space in a small, ten-man
shuttle. It's not luxurious, but not too shabby
either! The captain of the shuttle, Damien Affister,
is explaining to the navigator how to get average
speed. Suddenly, rocking. Computer banks
destroyed. We open the shutters. A wall of fire
and light.

Edward Hatfield (12)
Sevenoaks School

Fangs

Moonlight was her only candle as she slipped silently down the cobbled streets. Her only memory, the scream of her unsuspecting victim. Her newfound hunger driving her forward. End it now. No more pain, no more suffering, no more eternal thirst for blood. Do it. Just pull the trigger.

Edwina Low (13)
Sevenoaks School

Betrayal

I stared at what I'd done. Should I call the police?
There was no point. She was already dead. Blood
seeped from her chest. She wasn't breathing any
longer. Her body was limp. I took a step back.
How could I do it? How could I stab my best
friend?

Elysia Rothery (12)
Sevenoaks School

Forgotten And Dying

I lay there silently in the sinister darkness. There was a flickering light behind my closed eyelids. Gradually, the flickering became a deep glow. Sensing something was wrong, my bloodshot eyes burst open. A malevolent, menacing fire! The flaming creature pierced my skin. First, searing pain, then darkness engulfed me.

Amber Jeffryes (12)
Sevenoaks School

The Sleeping Castle

Never-ending cobwebs and a blanket of dust
- layer upon layer. The walls, strangled by
overgrown ivy, and people frozen in time. He
enters, in hope of reviving the sinister castle. Just
one kiss … servants leap into action and maids
clean away grime. The sleeping beauty, Princess
Aurora, has awoken!

Elizabeth Warwick-Champion (12)
Sevenoaks School

The Shot

Heart pounding, I stared into his fear-stricken eyes, hand trembling, my finger on the trigger. He sobbed, cried out his last plea and fell to the floor, weeping. Closing my eyes, I pulled the trigger. A sharp, everlasting crack whipped through the empty building. He lay there silent, motionless.

Katherine Edwards (12)
Sevenoaks School

203

Anne And The Blade

The dimly-lit candle had burned out gradually. My voice hoarse from excruciating screaming. *Whip!* My head was bruised and my neck throbbing. Only a few hours left with it … Sleep. Woken by rowdy babbling. The knife slashed. For ten seconds I was without body. Headless. Gone forever. Damn Henry.

Alice Grishkov (12)
Sevenoaks School

He Wasn't Lying

Our car crossed the corner. Nature ogling on the right and pollution on the left; adhered on the border of God's creation and Man's. Lip-red roses blooming in our direction, compared to the thick, black clouds overpowering habitats. Al Gore wasn't lying. Our car crashed, coincidentally on the left.

Benjamin Throsby (12)
Sevenoaks School

205

But I Don't Want To!

Mum asked, 'Will you empty the dishwasher?'
I answered, 'But I don't want to!'
Dad asked, 'Will you help me in the garden?'
I answered, 'But I don't want to!'
I helped them both anyway.
My sister asked, 'Will you go to a concert with me?'
I answered, *'Yes please!'*

Kate Stephen (12)
Sevenoaks School

An Innocent Killing

Not a word was spoken, it was as if the room was deserted. I lay on the ground, my cheek pressed against the chilled, impenetrable surface of the shop floor. The figure clenching the pistol aimed for the innocent man behind the till, like a farmer shooting a blameless rabbit.

Elle Watson (12)
Sevenoaks School

The Gunshots

The trees bow as I pass, while the other terrified animals flee with amazing speed. I accelerate, charging towards my goal. The wilderness becomes a blur around me. I reach maximum speed. I tense my muscles and spring, teeth bared. I crush my prey. The poacher's dying at my feet.

Sam Annetts (12)
Sevenoaks School

The Creature

Stumbling across the barren lands of Africa, running, never stopping for famine nor thirst, it was chasing him, mocking him. He was far from the village now. Away from safety, away from home. He fell down, he screamed. The nightmare was over. Famine had killed him. Death had caught him.

Liam Rock (13)
Sevenoaks School

The Price To Pay

There is blood on his sweater. The knife is sharp.
I am uneasy. I feel helpless as he lifts the blade,
the muscles in his arms rippling with strength.
The knife comes down. 'That'll be four pounds
fifty, Ma'am.' The butcher wraps the beef in
polystyrene before handing it over.

Zoe Brandon (13)
Sevenoaks School

The Game

My hand clutches the sword tight as I wander through the dark underground cave. The torch cuts through the air as I trudge through the swampy water. I hear a distant moan. Suddenly a huge, terrifying monster leaps out and roars, 'Clean your room before you go on your PlayStation!'

Jason Jiang (12)
Sevenoaks School

Gunshot

Bang! I sprinted towards the noise, weaving through the trees. I could see a faint outline. Trembling, I moved closer. Smothered with red. A cough came from his direction; he sat up. Unconvinced, I blinked. A boy ran past holding a gun with green, yellow and blue paintballs inside it.

Isabel Baldwin (12)
Sevenoaks School

Battle

Fearing the worst, I loaded my gun. I shuddered.
An abandoned car, sprayed with bullets, provided
cover. Smoke grenades created a thick fog,
allowing us to trudge through the mud, unseen.
With a loud gasp of pain, pink paint splattered
across my mask. I was out!

Liam Regan (14)

The Howard School

213

Dragon Rage

At the last chance I got, I climbed the dragon's
back, jumped on its head, got my sword, but it
shook and threw me metres. I ran back up it and,
'Turn that off,' said Mum.
'Do I have to?' I replied.
'Yes,' she said.
'OK then,' I replied back.

Matthew Askam (13)
The Howard School

Survival

Crawling through muddy terrain and weaving artillery fire, my heavy, rusty helmet slid down my soggy back. Black, hairy dogs barking around, ripping limbs off. I whipped out my heavy machine gun. I obliterated my opponent. Screaming in agony. Suddenly, 'Johnny, time to go! Turn your game off.'

Adam Fowler (13)
The Howard School

Burning Dream

The flames furiously whipped at the walls, leaving a trail of black smoke behind them. I ran, ducking and dodging the raw, red flames. I was sweating as the heat was unbearable. I thought this was the end for me! I jumped and landed in the comfort of my bed!

James Openshaw (14)
The Howard School

Tommy

Tommy was the best, better than the rest. Liked to kick a ball up against the wall. All he did now was play football.

One bright day, Tommy went to play because he was good. He had no friends in the hood. Then he turned bad, which made him sad.

Jack Phillips (13)
The Howard School

Holiday Adventures

'We have lift off,' said Rodney. Phillip was feeling
woozy as the plane had just scraped the clouds.
The hostess wheeled her cart and asked Rod,
'Are you interested in our dinner, sausage, mash,
beans?'
'Oh God, I'm gonna be sick!'
Eeaaiirgh! went Phil!
It was a furball. *Yuck!*

Ben Carwardine (13)

The Howard School

Attack

I was in a jeep, all the dust rushing up into my face. My team entered the central city. We were attacked. Our jeep was going 50mph. We were ambushed. I got out of the jeep and detached the 50 cal. *Boom!* as I pressed the X button.

Taylor Kelly (13)
The Howard School

The Battle Of Future And Past

As the Vikings' ships crossed the lock, the robots prepared for conflict. The Viking ships got ever closer. The robots opened fire. Balls of plasma flew in every direction As the Viking flanks failed to gain any land, the robots started to celebrate.
Victory was theirs.
'Come on Max, dinner!'

Lewis Middlewood (13)
The Howard School

The Evil Dentist

Jamie's bronze eyes glared into his mother's as he tried to persuade her that the local dentist is a monster that festers on children. She explained that the dentist helps children, but Jamie wouldn't believe her …
The next day Jamie went to the dentist, to find he's not so bad.

Harrison Marwaha (13)
The Howard School

221

The Battle To End All Battles

The dragon fumed in anger. He puffed smoke out of his nostrils then he lunged towards the armoured knight. The beast roared and spat out a line of bright fire. The knight leaped out of the way, ran up the monster's long tail ...
'Game over, you have lost!'

Manreeve Singh Dhothar (13)
The Howard School

The Chasing

I'm running as fast as I possibly can through the trees and the bushes. I can hear them getting closer, footsteps getting louder. My heart is beating faster. I trip over a branch. The footsteps stop, they must be here. All I hear is Jack shouting loudly, 'Tag! You're it!'

Omar Woodrow-Thorne (14)

The Howard School

The Explosion

Kaboom! I saw the man who'd captured the house, in a ball of flame. I called the police. It was *Blow-up Bill.* Bloody hell! And I got him! I collected the reward and went to Bluewater.
As soon as I got to the last checkout … I awoke in bed.

Damien Lacey (13)
The Howard School

Sprinting Rapidly, Falling Drastically

I jumped, I dodged, I skipped, I dived. Their footsteps were rapidly approaching. My legs could only run so fast and for so long. Sounds ricocheted past my ears. Skidding into a nearby alley, I slipped! Scrambling for my feet, I was ripped viciously to the ground. Ripped to Hell!

Matt Roper (14)

The Howard School

225

The End

'Why are you driving at such tempo?' Bella's eyes were glued to the road. Cold and shaky, she checked the rear-view mirror. I swiftly realised that we were being stalked. The tyres screeched. We were hit. *Bang!* We crashed, never to wake again.

'What a pathetic story!' exclaimed Matthew.

Sam Richman (13)

The Howard School

The Morning

The barrage of gunfire fills the grey sky. It's enough to make any man insane. Dark red blood engulfs the floor, staining my torn, crimson-red uniform. A blast powerfully ruptures my arm's vein! Blood pours ...

Suddenly I'm in a warm room. A familiar voice murmurs, 'Wake up, honey.'

Goran Jovanovski (13)
The Howard School

The Creeping Night

Stumbling out the club, drunk and disorderly, she hobbles over the creaking bridge. Then footsteps … creeping closer, closer. She panics. The footsteps suddenly stop. She looks behind her. Nothing! She stares closer. In the murky alleyway are two white eyes! She screams, 'Don't hurt me!' 'Sorry, you forgot your coat.'

Lisle Twitchett (14)
The Howard School

Dodgeball Match

He was running from the fear of death, dodging everything that they threw at him. He couldn't escape; they wouldn't stop. He couldn't breathe. There was no time, they'd get him. He picked up the dodgeball and threw it back. His face lit up - he had got someone!

James Sivyer (13)
The Howard School

The Dentist

Machines were going off. They pinned me down and started to attack. They shone a bright light into my eyes, blinding me. They had sharp tools, threatening murder. They put a needle inside me, knocking me out. Afterwards, when I came to, the dentist said, 'See you next week.'

Taylor Parbutt
The Howard School

The Weird Café

I was dawdling along the road when I saw a café. I stepped into it. The lights were off. Footsteps got closer and closer. I saw zombies! I tiptoed slowly backwards. The zombies were walking towards me and one of them moaned, 'May I take your order, Sir?'

Kyle Bryce (13)
The Howard School

The Evil Dentist

I lay there in the blue chair. Next to me lay kinds of silver weapons, dripping with other patients' blood. A light beamed down on me. A masked man was staring at his computer. I was incredibly terrified at this point. Then the masked man asked, 'Open wide please, Sir.'

Sean Hawkins (13)
The Howard School

The Waiting Room

The room was dull - white walls, ripped magazines on a wooden table in the centre of the grey carpet. I sat hoping I wouldn't be next. I stared at the speaker in the dreary room, hoping it wouldn't call for me. The speaker called my name. The dentist came.

Jack Smith (13)
The Howard School

233

The Monster

She stood there, growling at whoever dared speak. The room fell silent as she looked for her first victim. She slithered over to me, giving me that evil look. She grabbed my page and struck it. Her face went red with anger. 'Billy, this is your worst work ever!'

Kieran Weston (13)

The Howard School

The Deep

Taking a large gulp of air, I threw myself into the water, diving below. Dark shadows loomed. An eerie echoing grew louder and louder. I had to get out. Rushing upwards I gasped for air, my head breaking the surface.
'Get out of the bath. You look like a prune!'

Bradley Mercer (13)
The Howard School

The War

I was the last man alive. Three enemy ships
unloaded thousands of the small, grunting
creatures. I paused. They surrounded me. Barking
noises filled the air. I shot my guns, pulling them
off my belt. Bolts of plasma screamed towards
me. Everything went black. I had run out of
credit.

Philip Andrew (13)
The Howard School

The Cure

Sneaking through the uninhabited crop plantation, black hood up, he proceeds through the open window, tripping the alarm. The sirens wail! Snatching the test tube - the ultimate prize - he retreats, making a hasty escape. Drinking the liquid, he knows soon enough he'll be human.

George Diamond (13)
The Howard School

Untitled

The skies darkened. An uproar came from the
submerged cave. As flames roared, he took
the challenge. With the smell of the beast
overwhelming, the horse became agitated and
fled. In to combat with the furious beast he went.
Soon blood spurted from the creature's heart.
Wow! Another level won!

Scott Theobald (13)
The Howard School

Burn In Hell

Roland woke up on the scorching ash, flames licking his face. He had to move on. Roars were gradually creeping closer. Managing to scramble to his feet, Roland limped forwards. The flames towered above him. He was so close, but flames surrounded him and he let them engulf his body.

Stephen Fishman (14)
The Howard School

The Game

The roar of machine guns deafens my ears. We advance up the battlefield towards enemy lines. Bullets flying everywhere, miss their targets. Then smoke engulfs the air, covering our eyes. *Bang! Bang!* Two bullets in the head. Blood blinds my eyes …

'Oh my God! That game was amazing!'

Bradley Webb (14)
The Howard School

The Battle

Grimbos attacking left and right, their scaly skin oozed slime from every pore. My sergeant reduced to ashes in front of my eyes. We were surrounded. Bullets ricocheted everywhere, it was hopeless. We made our final stand. I snatched a grenade and ripped off the pin, springing towards the enemy …

Lewis Rowe (14)
The Howard School

Vampire Attack

'Argh!' Vampires circled us viciously like wolves. We were in the gloomy forest. We hunched up together and we waited forever, then we broke up in terror. They attacked me barbarically. My friends were being ripped apart. I saw a flash of gold light, then there was nothing … except darkness.

Adem Bal (13)
The Howard School

Untitled

'I want the money, *now!*' demanded the masked man. 'Don't delay me, give it!' Revealing the shiny grey object, he yelled, 'Don't test me!' *Bang!* The banker collapsed to the floor. Blood oozed from the open wound and swam across the marble floor.

'And cut!' screamed the director.

Christopher Billingham (13)
The Howard School

Untitled

We pulled up outside the building. He pushed me inside, then slammed the door shut. They shoved me into a leather chair. Pulling out a pair of sharp razors, he hurried towards me. I felt the blade slide across my neck. 'How short do you want it?' he asked.

Daniel Owen (13)
The Howard School

The Darkness

It looked at me with its fiery red eyes and the dark, jagged black cloak it was dragging behind it. It pulled out a glistening blade, shining in its beauty. I could see it in the flickering light above me. *Slash!* I was destroyed.
'Game over,' the computer said.

Harry Prebble (14)
The Howard School

Battleships

Zap! Ship one is destroyed. 'One down, two to
go,' mumbled the pilot. *Zoom!* Shoots off the
missile, dead on ship two. 'Yes! Last one to go,'
the pilot joyfully sang. *Boom!* Game over.
'No, I've lost the game. Now my life is over,'
cried John after losing his game.

Sheraz Hussain (14)

The Howard School

Game Over

Avoiding death, missiles blaze past me as I frantically search for shelter amongst the crumbling buildings. Launching myself behind a wall, I narrowly missed a bullet. Silence. Dare I peek? *Bang!* I'm hit between the eyes, lying in a pool of blood. It fades to black.

Game over.

Daniel Hurst (14)
The Howard School

Curious, Curious Animal

Curious, curious animal scuttled everywhere.
It was mysterious and extremely stealthy. The
animal valued food. It always slipped and glided
to every tree. The tree of gold appeared in front
of the stunned animal. Running and jumping, the
animal urgently climbed to the golden bananas.
Suddenly, *ooh, ooh, aah, aah*.

Aaron Hussain (13)
The Howard School

Trying To Evade

Thundering like an arrow, I tried to evade the
agile troll getting closer and closer. I wouldn't
abandon my gold, I'd risked too much. Tumbling
over, I snapped around quickly, only to find the
thing bellowing over me.
'Alright son, you're nicked,' the policeman roared.

Ross Baker (13)
The Howard School

249

Untitled

I could hear a blade being sharpened as heavy footsteps came closer. Frozen still, I screamed. No reply. I was alone. I turned my head to the right and saw the masked man's eyes glaring at me, with a blade in his hand.
'Do you like your new hair?'

Cieran McNamee (14)
The Howard School

The Game

Blistering sunlight shone down onto the abandoned street. Bare, dead trees littered the pathway. Turning down a gloomy alleyway, the police gained on me. A dead end. Humungous police vehicles sped towards me. I couldn't move! 'My spacebar doesn't work!' I shouted out, noticing the screen displayed *Game Over!*

Edward Johnson (13)
The Howard School

No One Is Left Behind

Mexican backstreets, the jungle of the city, were the home to the greatest masterminds. Pte Rodrigez silently trekked forward, his M4 pressed against his sweaty, camouflaged cheek. A bullet descending, ripped through his leg. Heroically he crawled to cover …

'For the last time, turn it off!' screamed Mum from downstairs.

Brandon Dixey (13)
The Howard School

The Exam

Time is not on my side. No one wants to be
in this building but it's for my own good. Rain
smashes on the building's windows. Stern stares
watch my every move. Time is running out. What
am I going to do?
'Put down your pens. Your test is over.'

Aaron Brookes (13)
The Howard School

Terror At The Dentist

We all lined up, waiting for the torture to begin.
Cries of agony echoed around the room. I stood
in anticipation, tapping my fingers. A man burst
out of one of the doors, clutching his jaw in
anguish. 'Mr Mehmed, it's time for your dental
check up.'

Alex Peters (13)

The Howard School

The Game

His heart pounded as he crept into darkness.
Sweat trickled into his body kit. Holding his gun
with such grip, he proceeded onwards. Ringing
in his ear was the sound of rain and then those
words, those dreadful words, 'Dinner's ready!
Stop playing that game.'
Sighing, he dropped the controller.

Thomas Baker (13)
The Howard School

High Up

I climbed the ladder, forced forward by the man
behind. I tried to get down but he just kept
pushing me. My knees trembled. I looked down,
the water rippled. I fell back. He threw me.
Smack!
'Good, now you've jumped, try diving,' my diving
instructor said.

William Mayger (13)
The Howard School

The Plane

The plane soared through the air, bolting past
the enormous black clouds, swerving in and out,
dodging bullets. He was demolishing gun ships,
watching them sink hopelessly into the sea.
Bullets pounded into his right wing. 'I'm hit!'
'John, get out of the bath. Stop playing around.'

Jack Currie (13)
The Howard School

The Chase

My breath was failing. A pair of devious eyes glared at me as a large figure sprinted rapidly towards me. My heart jumped out of my body. I had to get past it. I ran as quickly as I could, got past the defender and tapped in a stunning goal.

Ayyaz Mehmood (14)
The Howard School

The Monster

The wind blew against the window. The creature was near. It mustn't find me. I silently moved across the dark wall toward the light switch. Thinking I could startle the monster with light I turned it on, but found out the monster was only Dad.

Freddie Batchelor (13)

The Howard School

Untitled

The roar of the screaming animals sent shivers down my spine. 'It has to end.' Then I saw him, a wild glare in his eyes. I trembled as he approached, faster and closer, gaining on me every second. I had few options left. Terrified, I took the shot and scored.

Jake Kavanagh (13)
The Howard School

45 Minutes

The orange, fiery walls created such an overpowering heat, sweat dripped gradually down my cheeks and onto my shirt. I grew weary, my breathing got heavier and heavier. On the verge of falling asleep a voice spoke. 'OK, Tom, you can go now. Your DT is over,' said Miss Tomris!

Thomas Doran (13)
The Howard School

Untitled

Wind rushed past my face as I plummeted
towards the earth. I was thrown back in my seat
as the force tied me down. I knew my journey
was over. My life was about to end. The world
went blank.
'Mum! I need 50p more!'

Matt Parker (13)
The Howard School

The Roller Coaster

The wind rushing past my hair, the G-force
crushing on my chest, screaming from all over
the place. As we gently stopped my mum asked,
'How'd you like the roller coaster?'

Rhys Parker (14)
The Howard School

Untitled

Sweat dripped down his face. Until now, he had overcome all obstacles. He had shown off his skills under the watchful eyes of the audience. Surely nothing would stop him on his way to glory? Nervously he looked up, horror in his eyes. It was science - his worst subject.

Charlie Sweatman (14)
The Howard School

The Landing

Thump! We had arrived. Months of lonely drifting, now we're here. A world of dull craters awaited me. The radio screamed in my head. The door opened. A bleak landscape stared us down. Black sky lingered overhead. Stars winked cheekily. 'One small step for me, one giant leap for mankind!'

Kieron Morgan (14)
The Howard School

Escape

Eeeer, bang! Bang! Bang! It breaks through. It looks at me with its dark, blood-filled eyes and the remains of its last victim still in its mouth. I know that if I don't escape, I could be its next victim. I must escape. I must!

Ashley Purvis (13)
The Howard School

Untitled

A killer. A deadly virus. It's fight or death. You will not survive. It will jump out at you. This is the end of the world. This all happened on my laptop.

Liam Wickson (13)

The Howard School

The Visit ...

She smiled, revealing her crooked yellow teeth.
The mirror reflected people staring closely.
Razors got closer and got louder, causing me to
shudder. Couldn't she see the terror on my pale
face? A black apron covered me, red stains visible.
Is she a murderer? Suddenly ...
'Blonde highlights?' exclaimed the hairdresser.

Sam Rodger (13)
The Howard School

The Modern Warfare

Impishly I walked on the battlefield, leaves running wildly and trees undressed. The modern warfare began. Darting bullets came flying towards me. I took cover. My gun jammed, my enemies closed in. A bullet hit me. Red liquid stained my sweatshirt unpleasantly. A voice cheered, 'Nice paint stain, mate!'

Scott Trenton (14)
The Howard School

Brutal Butcher

I violently kill my prey at the dead of night, drag
the blood-smeared corpses to my van.
At the destination, I firmly grasp my bloodthirsty
knife, chop off all the limbs. Precision is essential.
As I hang up the parts …
'One rack of pork ribs,' says the customer.

Jordan Murphy (13)
The Howard School

The Bad One!

Raising his head, John takes a deep breath. He
starts to mutter strangely to himself, pulling
himself up. Swaying, he straightens himself,
leaning on a tree. He hears a shout which bursts
his eardrums. He springs, running through the
wood …
'Wake up, John, you were just having a bad
dream.'

Dominic Harris (13)
The Howard School

Untitled

Sitting in the dark chair, moving would be a big mistake. Sweating like a pig, it was pouring down my forehead, off the tip of my nose. Sharp metal blades everywhere around me. Nobody would like to be where I am now. 'Mohican, please.' He snipped away at my hair.

Ryan Austin (13)
The Howard School

Mini Marvels Kent

The Christmas Slaughterhouse

As the crooked man opened the shed door, the rain marched them inside the shack. They knew they wouldn't return. Lightning showed flashing shadows of men launching axes down. Every time an axe was thrown, one less turkey could be heard. Outside, Sainsbury's lorries waited. It was Christmas.

Chris Rowles (13)

The Howard School

Halloween!

Groaning filled the air and as he turned around,
he suddenly realised that he was surrounded
by hungry-looking creatures. Jimmy tried not
to vomit as blood and saliva dripped from their
mouths and dead skin seeped from their battered
clothes. Something tapped him on his back. 'Trick
or treat?'

Josh Barnes (14)
The Howard School

The Terrifying Night

In my bleak bedroom, a light from outside
illuminated my bedroom wall. Suddenly dark,
evil-looking shadows appeared upon my wall,
the shape of devils. Were they real or were they
coming from outside? I peered out of my window.
It was only the Halloweeners.

Ethan Britchfield (13)
The Howard School

The Final Blow

I kicked, I jumped, sprinted and dodged. I could
hear the deep panting coming from behind me.
I turned once, twice, but the third I could not.
Then I took that one final blow. To my excitement
it was enough. England had once again reclaimed
the World Cup!

Freeman Rogers (14)

The Howard School

Hide-And-Seek

Sprinting through bushes, I was covered in cuts.
People were staring. I knew they were catching
up - I had to think fast. With my heart pounding, I
ran into the gloomy forest, looking for a way out.
I quickly hid behind a towering tree.
'Tag, you're on,' shouted Regan happily.

Christopher Harvey (13)
The Howard School

The Ten Chicks

There was a little girl called Aqua. She had seven reindeer. She went for a swim. She saw a great white shark and her nose started to grow. It killed the shark, as she was telling lies about her reindeer. Really she only had ten ugly, bald chicks.

Cameron Thomas (13)
The Howard School

The Beast!

Gasping for air, I ran through the house trying to get away from the bloodthirsty beast. Its red eyes were fixed on me. I felt so scared. It was gaining on me. I knew it was the end. It pounced. 'Get off me, you silly old dog!'

Joshua Rose (13)
The Howard School

Haunted House Horror

It calls out to me as I inch past. Chris crawls closer to the gaping door. The creaky floorboards splinter as we fall towards the basement. A moist red substance glares from the slick blades. I stare. His motionless body lies mutilated. I stand still, I'm paralysed with fear.

Steven Coote (13)
The Howard School

Mystery Meal

The razor-sharp knife easily cut through the flesh.
It was dark and it was late at night and a smell
lingered in the air. He washed his hands to get rid
of the evidence. He then put the corpse in the
oven and said, 'Dinner will be 20 minutes.'

Ryan Holmes (14)
The Howard School

Prison Cell

Jeremy met a girl down an alley. He really liked
her, she was called Jess. So they carried on seeing
each other, drinking and going clubbing. They
decided that they wanted to spend their lives
together. They bought a house. Then they found
themselves in prison cells.

Matt Clewes

The Howard School

Catapult War

I took a shot on the chest. I hid behind a tree,
trying to relocate my target. As I lined up my
target, he quickly hid behind a bush. I reloaded
and laughed as I heard someone fart. Suddenly,
again, my target appeared. *Bang!* The game of
catapults was over!

Scott Clark (14)

The Howard School

Graveyard Mystery

I was walking with my family to the extraordinary graveyard, when two people behind me burst out crying. I turned round. They were twins. Blond hair, blue eyes. I looked behind them and there was a coffin. Then suddenly I realised, horses were taking the coffin to the graveyard. Why?

Sam Barnden (13)
The Howard School

Jack And Jill

Jack and Jill went up the hill to vote for their respected parties. Despite what they had agreed, Jack still voted for Conservatives. Jill, in blind rage, snapped Jack's crown, pushed him down and demanded an explanation to why he actually likes Gordon Brown!

Javier Tucker (17)

West Kent College

She Always Loved To Dance

The dark room paid silent witness, illuminated soft, sickly yellow by a patient streetlamp. It was then she saw the broken figure, dancing mournfully to a hollow song. Dr Napier would be sad, the medication was ineffective. She settled in alone, save the spectre of her loving, long dead mother.

Stephen Hall (17)
West Kent College

My Alter Ego

'Sasha,' said a loud female voice. It was a voice I couldn't recognise. It made me want to talk back to it and most nights, for no apparent reason, I would wake up because all I can hear was this annoying, tedious voice buzzing around my head. Twisted? Psychotic? Demented?

Dorothy Musariri (17)
West Kent College

I Need A Hero

The moors of Dunville were graced with a ghostly presence. The beautiful, tall figure emerged, riding gallantly and fearlessly. Hunting those who had wronged him, he searched for his tormentors, delivering justice wherever possible. Like the town's protector, he could be depended on, always …
She awoke, wishing he was real.

Nikita Chadha (17)
West Kent College

A Day In The Life Of 'Other Pig'

Five years since the wolf … the house remained.
Since then … insurance, credit cards: reality.
'Worker pig' and 'undervalued housewife pig'
were arguing. The cracks in their civil partnership
were showing. 'Other pig' had had enough; a
fairy-tale pig in modern society … loneliness. He
picked up a knife, again - pondering …

Joshua Perez-Del-Pulgar-Cole (17)
West Kent College

The Ravenous Ravens

Upon their jagged perch, a conspiracy of ravens keep their mark under vigilant surveillance. A lone vole scurries along the rugged, unkempt ground of the venerable Palladian manor. The cabal of ravens sensing their opportunities, strike. By now, the vole is little more than carrion, and is to move nevermore.

Luke South (16)
West Kent College

The Assassination

The assassin breathed deeply and slowly, his eyes glued to the rifle scope. He waited atop a tall building, lining up the crosshair to his foe. The target's head lay unprotected. A clean shot. His finger tightened on the trigger. *Bang! Game Over.* Joe sighed. He had one life left.

Samuel Bassett (18)
West Kent College

291

Hide-In-Sheep

Another summer's day. The pigs and sheep
decided to play a game. The pigs went to get
their blankets … well, all but one!
Time passed … but that one wasn't found. In the
field was fur. Slowly pulling it back, revealing the
pig. He thought they were playing hide-in-sheep.

Lee Concannon (17)
West Kent College

Just Another Day ...

The sound of dustmen wakes me. Another day on the streets. My stomach rumbles. I haven't eaten properly in days. I look at the people walking past. Some take pity, others spit and make jokes. Soon I'll have enough for food, but not now. I'm starving. I'm cold. Please help.

Jonathan Griffin (18)
West Kent College

293

The Legend Of Victorious Valhala

Shut my eyes, lay down to rest. My small village
girl still breathing next to me. Dirt topples, closing
in. My eyes burst open, panic closes my throat.
I fall aimlessly towards Summery Fall, bitter ale
and booming men. Horses neighing softly; angelic
voices floating gently. I finally feel alive.

Georgina Bennett (16)
West Kent College

Kevin And James Got Hungry

The sheep, Kevin and James, found a broken
fence in a time where the air was rather dense.
The farmer had not yet noticed, for on watch he
had not been posted. The cabbage was gone, lost
in Kevin's tum and so then, for dinner, the farmer
just got thinner.

Josef Hills (17)
West Kent College

Like Cat And Mouse

It's bright outside. Hunger paws at her belly as she tentatively steps outside. Sunlight washes over her. Her nose twitches at the scent of food. Her oil-drop eyes fix on the grain, scent tempting her forward. Pink paws patter against the hard ground. Then, a shadow. A weight. Black.

Annabel Abraham (17)

West Kent College

A White Mystery

There once was a man called Dan, who drove a big white van. He fixed everyone's cars for cheap - from new ones to ones that belong in a heap. He thought he was doing right, but he was as dark as night. He drove up and down - killing around town.

Craig Giles (18)
West Kent College

Information

We hope you have enjoyed reading this book - and that you will continue to enjoy it in the coming years.

If you like reading and writing, drop us a line or give us a call and we'll send you a free information pack. Alternatively visit our website at **www.youngwriters.co.uk**

Write to:

Young Writers Information,
Remus House,
Coltsfoot Drive,
Peterborough,
PE2 9JX

Tel: (01733) 890066
Email: youngwriters@forwardpress.co.uk